Thoughts of you

First Printing: 2022
Written and reproduced by SMR
Cover Illustration: Credit to drawing creator

ISBN: 9798847587426
Imprint: Independently published

Thoughts of you

Written by: SMR

Dedicated to love

in every way, shape, and form

Past or present

My heart is yours

She

There once was a girl,
she was beautiful
everything about her was.
She was as sweet as honey,
the bees must have worked hard on her.
She smelled of daisies
I would only hope to have walked through those fields that she, herself, thrived upon.
Her smile was like sunshine itself,
it would light up the whole world if it could.
She was the galaxy,
with its fires ablaze and dancing colors.
She was and is anything and everything.

Considering Myself A Writer This One Time

As a writer
you know certain things come easy,
to jot down,
to think of
and being capable of blabbing on and on about said thing,
but,
they don't tell you
when you meet the one
that you're speechless.
unable to comprehend language;
forming into a writer's block,
not because you can't write about them
but
because you are so overwhelmed
with emotion and these small words;
that nothing else seems to match
the sensation you get when you look into their eyes
no language could ever describe
the rhythm their heart makes
when you're near them.
It's just so awfully difficult to explain;
that I can only hope you too
can feel it for yourself.

Everyday
I sit back
and try to think of the right words to describe
how I feel.
I ponder the English language
and realize that none of these words,
on the tip of my tongue,
taste right.
I'm lost in a sea of emotions towards you
and I'm not drowning,
but I am a boat
sailing to where your love is
and it's incredible.

Since you've come into my life,
I have known peace

-Thank You

Wildflower

You are the fields of wildflowers
that the sun shines down upon,
day after day,
to make sure they can grow,
the ones the rain drips down on so they will be fed,
the ones where the dirt is soft but stay firm to protect the roots
that lay beneath
because they realize what they are protecting is the most
beautiful thing they've ever seen
and they will do all they can to make
sure they are loved and safe in this world;
You are my wildflower,
I am
the sun,
the rain,
and the dirt.

I used to think I had bad luck until I met you

Touch

I don't want anyone else's fingerprints carved into the pores of my skin;
I want the imprint of the marks surrounding your fingers across my body;
I want the skin to remember
the designs your fingerprints hold;
the designs that mark mine were meant for yours to intertwine;
It fits perfectly into the swirl of creases along
the edges of my back;
and when our fingertips touch you can feel them lock
and then the energy flows through us to our hearts
which have their own designs,
where only two can make one;
So let our fingerprints lock and combine;
So I'll hold my hand out if you allow yourself to do the same

1/3

In another universe far away,
we are together every day
I wake up each morning
to you rubbing the sleep from your eyes
as I gently lay a kiss upon your cheek.
In another universe
I get to hold your hand at every grocery store we walk into
In another universe
there isn't a second that goes by
where I am not by your side,
it may sound selfish
but in another universe
I have you near in every waking second and nothing is wasted.

2/3

In this universe
you are far away.
I roll over in the morning
hoping I went to sleep with you there the night before.
In this universe
I wish I could walk into the next room
and tuck the hair falling into your face behind your ears
and kiss your cheek.
In this universe
I long for the seconds in your arms.
In this universe
I make sure I give you my all
because you deserve the galaxy
In this universe
I make sure the seconds we do get together or apart
are not wasted.

3/3

In every universe,
we find our way to one another
and nothing is
nor will ever be
wasted.

Standing here at the edge of my bed
staring at the place you once laid,
Makes my heart feel weary,
even possibly dreary;
I find myself staring at every thing you've touched
everything you've left your mark on
I begin to picture you there
and everything in me wants to run;
run to where you are;
run to where you stay,
just to catch a glimpse of your face
and know it is okay
to remember you like this,
to relive these moments
and know that one day
I'll be standing at the edge of my bed
staring straight at
you.

Voice

I know you say you hate your voice
and ask why I do not;
but all I can think about is how the words roll off your tongue
and how the pitch changes when you get excited
or with every tone it blends into a song yet to be sung;
Oh how miraculous it sounds when you say my name,
or any word at that
It's the only sound that I'd be content hearing everyday
until I cease to exist
just know
It's just as wonderful as you are

Stars

There's only one thing
I love more than the stars
and
It's you

Time

Every year
every day
every hour
every second
I will give to you
Time can't measure the love I have for you
If it stopped,
that wouldn't stop me
from counting the moments
until I could hold you again
I'd count every nonexistent second
until I heard your voice
once more

Soulmate

Finding you so young
is a blessing and a curse
We love recklessly
hope fiercely
You see this can be risky
we could lose everything we thought we had
but could gain everything we never imagined to be true
With you in this moment
in this life
it feels like I'm discovering the secrets of the oceans
the planets beyond the stars
these oceans
these stars
They live inside of you
You're made from them and
I have dedicated my life to my passion
that passion lies
within you

What You Deserve

You deserve the warmth of the summer winds,
and the rainbows after a storm
You deserve the stars to shine for eternity,
just to light your paths and your journeys;
You deserve more love than I can give,
the never-ending love of the universe;
I am not the universe but
I will gather up the stars
and the light of the sun
just to put it in a bag
and offer it to you
because you deserve
the earth
the sun,
the moon;
You deserve love.

Near

Could you imagine if you were here,
How it'd feel
How you'd look
Can you hear the rhythms of our hearts beating,
side by side;
Feel the warmth of my touch on your skin,
Hearing our voices chime in together,
nearer and nearer
is where I long to be
Near you,
for always

No One Ever Could

There is no one on this planet,
that could love me the way you do;
No one could sound as sweet saying my name;
They couldn't make my heart beat out of its cage,
or stretch my smile from ear to ear;
You fill my life with so much joy
like no one ever could

Angel

Heaven must be real,
I mean it must be,
if they sent you here;
You must have floated down from the clouds,
landing softly on your feet,
only to bring grace,
love,
and kindness
to wash away the past
to brighten the future
It had to have brought you here to me

Older

There are times I wish we were older,
Old enough to be on our own,
to do our own thing;
It seems to make everything more promising;
We could do whatever our hearts desired;
We could find happiness in the everyday things,
Nothing could hold us back
No one could,
If we were older;
but I won't wish away our youth,
We'll get there one day

If

If this were the last time I would ever see you again
I'd want you to know,
that this love will last a lifetime
That you were the most pristine being
I've ever laid my eyes on;
the carvings of your face
will never unhinge itself
from my minds eye;
If I could never lay a kiss upon your lips again
you should know they set fireworks off in my heart,
in my chest,
my life;
If this was it,
just know,
everything was for you,
I regret nothing

You are just as beautiful as the art you create;
possibly even more

Fate

Say we never met
and we were someone else,
That wouldn't stop me from scavenging
the Earth,
land,
and sea
calling out the familiar name
that I know not of;
It would not dim the stars
that shine a pathway to your heart
nor
would it cease the wind
that blows in your direction,
leading me right to your door;
Say we never met,
Fate would still call

My Light

As I stand here admiring the details of your face,
I realize there was never a purer moment than this;
My hands don't shake,
my chest doesn't hurt
I have never been so calm;
The only thought that weighs on my mind
is how much I care about you;
My heart is full and now there is light

August 23, 2013

"I wish I had someone to count the stars with…
to trace the constellations on the back of my hand."

2015/2016

Every constellation, every single star in the sky has been traced on my hand various times, these constellations have absorbed into my blood stream and traveled to my heart,
I'm overflowing with the stars light;
I now can shine brighter than the moon
because of you

First Glance

My mind still rings
with the images of seeing your face
for the first time

The Rest Of My Days

I want the porch sitting,
hand holding kind of future
I want the fall down and you try to lend me a hand
but you just fall too
because our knees are too
brittle and weak;
I want grandkids telling me the impact of our love
even after our souls no longer walk this Earth;
Those days are the ones I hope for
side by side
hand in hand
with no one but you

Battle

When my heart races with urgency,
my mind clouds
my lungs thicken,
I can't catch my breath,
You're there to guide me through the fog,
to settle my heart's pattern,
to help me fight the fight;
You're there for every battle;
I will always do the same for you

Sunsets

Every sunset I see,
will only remind me of thee

My brain still hasn’t comprehended
that someone like you is in my life

Because Of You

Facing my fears does not seem as frightening now

I will never stop dreaming of you

Directions

Unzip my skin, reach for my heart
Hold it and secure it tight
Unleash yours, let it shine;
Place beneath my ribs
Now I have yours,
You have mine

This is what I was waiting for

Apologies

I am sorry
I let my heart grow envious
of those who can surround themselves of you daily,
I just long for that privilege

My bed doesn't feel like it used to
before you laid in it,
It’s now just lifeless,
cold,
empty

I would rather be waking up next to you

I am apathetic to this city,
but for you,
I am willing to stay

Just know
I'd move to the middle of the ocean
as long as it was near to you

-Anywhere For You

Goodbye feels too final,
So let's just always leave it at
a see you later

-Later Gator

Jump In

Let your soul unwind,
cradled in my arms
Unravel your heart
let my warm hands
sort out the pieces,
Revealing the soul beneath my bones
has never felt so peaceful,
so calm,
so right;
Jump into the sky with me;
Darling let's float down to the seas,
find a boat
and adventure the Earth;
While our purpose is right beside us,
Just you and I

You are more than enough

When your heart's filled up with the harsh emotions
of last year;
when it feels like it's going to burst
into a million pieces
across the floor;
When everything is just too much to handle,
Just let it go, show me your core
I promise I will be there
to collect your brittle bones
and glue them back into the person you are now
You grow,
You change,
the past doesn't make you who you are
if you do not want it to, but
I will be here even if you let it
I will be here

-Always

Fifty years beside you would be a blessing

Last

They say first loves last forever,
They are wrong about first loves;
The first had no comparison to this,
While you were not my first foolish love,
You are my last.
You have taught me what love actually is;
My forever

Looks of disgust,
Wide-eyed stares
Sly hateful whispering
All from passersby,
who happen to know nothing of us;
Not our names
Our favorite colors
anything
but still they let their hearts judge from who we love
It’s okay though,
I don’t mind what they think they know
as long as you hold my hand,
as I get lost in the greatest love I’ve ever known

-I Don't Mind

Thank you for loving even the darkest pieces of me

Online

I've gotten to know your depths
before I've ever seen you
Getting to know someone,
the real person beneath,
Before you can judge their physical attributes
is one of the more incredible experiences in life
You're not going in blind,
because your heart has eyes of it's own
that sees into the hearts and souls of others
before your eyes can see for themselves,
I have fallen in love with your love
your soul
your mind
It is in the truest forms of love

You make me a better person

Every foolish love song now makes sense

How I long to be in your presence

Risk

I will always keep you from harm
Your life comes before mine
I will jump in front of danger in an attempt
to even possibly save you from whatever may come;
I'd risk it all
for you

Storm

My heart beats with the sound of your name;
Echoing through my chest like a thunderstorm;
Lightning strikes,
one by one,
Brighter and more passionate with each strike,
each looks towards you;
You are a storm in my life
and it's so calming

Timeless

As you lay in bed,
beside me,
my mind starts to realize,
time and the future
Of how complicated it could be;
Then my hand traces your back once more;
I take notice of the calmness,
how time feels altered in the moments
I'm with you;
That it almost merely ceases to exist,
Maybe it's because I simply don't want it to,
So I am able to fill the timeless space with you here,
next to me
or because when two people have each other,
time feels what they have
and offers a small helping hand
just to make sure we all have enough time

Wonderful/Beautiful

You fill my arms and the empty spaces within my heart,
Your love is the everlasting glow
and the warmth spread among faces;
You make everything so bright and beautiful
It's as if this damned world is whole and wonderful
in fact perfect once more;
It's as if no harm will come to us because time stops when I look into your eyes,
the more I look the deeper I fall in love
with the person you were,
the person you are
and the person you will become;
Every waking minute with you is an infinity in paradise
and in that moment I feel whole,
able,
put back together;
You are my other half
My wonderful, beautiful girl

Not even gravity could pull my heart from loving you

Honesty

Honestly
I am lost in this life;
I don't know what I want
or where I'm going;
Who knows where I will be in 10 years
what I'll be wearing
what car I'll drive
but all I know is that I see you there
and none of the other stuff really matters;
The only thing that makes sense is you
and if that's all I will have
then I am and will be
perfectly content with this life

Seeds

There are seeds that you planted inside my heart;
The flowers that bloom from them
wrap lightly around my lungs
and entangle my ribs,
Each individually,
They're beautiful
and they smell like you;
I have a garden growing beneath my skin;
I hope you never forget to water it

It's A Big Deal

To others,
one night of texting,
one night of calling,
one night of video chatting
seems like the equivalent to an in-person interaction
but to us,
the people who know firsthand,
one night of missing any of those things is a big deal
and completely not the equivalent of being by their side;
No calls or messages could ever be close
to touching their skin,
feeling their warm breath against your neck,
or staring straight into their eyes;
It's not the same
so don't listen when they say you're naive
or that it's not a big deal
because they are the naive ones,
they don't know how it feels
to be so far
from your favorite beating heart

If there are ever doubts floating through your mind,
plaguing your heart;
I want you to read the words
etched into this book
To know that you are loved
and I will never stop caring for you

I have never felt this way about
another human being before;
You are different;
You are what gets me through life;
I couldn't dare ask for more;
You are more than enough

If I ever get mad,
please don't be sad
I won't mean to get annoyed,
it will most likely be me;
Sometimes I'm cranky,
sometimes I'm tired
and words don't want to come out of my mouth;
Sometimes I'm stubborn and won't listen,
sometimes I do things without thinking;
My annoyance doesn't link to you,
it links to life
and if I'm ever annoyed don't doubt who you are or where we are or how I feel for you,
If I'm ever crabby just know it's me
and my problems
That I still love you,
want you
and care for you;
Please don't worry,
Please don't doubt,
Please don't be sad,
Please just wait it out and know it's just a mood

I love you now and I'll love you then

You are the only one

Someone like you is the reason why I waited

Sunset

And when the sun sets,
my mind's still with you

I now know why nothing ever worked out before

-You Are Why

Echo

The mountains have echoed my name
since I was younger,
I want to be among them and free
But even if I lived in a boat
out in the middle of the Atlantic
as long as you'd be there,
the sea would begin to call out my name
as long as you'd call it too

May 5th, 2016

Time keeps moving,
very,
very quickly;
It feels I've met you only just yesterday,
yet the feeling of having known you for years is present;
The feeling of newness and familiarity combine,
into a perfect blend;
It's been six months of the hard work
and dedication
we've both poured into each other;
I am so thankful you've decided to light up my world,
while I keep yours spinning

Heart Eyes

You deserve
to be the happiest you've ever been
every second
of your entire life

Infinite Skies

I hope you dream of the stars
and traveling beyond the galaxies;
to touch a ray of light
with the glow that radiates from your soul
It demands to be seen
by those who can appreciate genuine beauty;
May your dreams gift you
with the engulfing happiness the world creates for you
Don’t let the dreams attack your heart,
let them lift you up
and use them to soar into the
infinite skies

If I could live in a moment;
I'd choose every one that I've had with you

The Days Following Christmas

I'll never forget the first time I saw you standing there,
your back against the wall,
that hazel green glint in your eyes;
Soft and nervous,
I could see the emotions dancing upon your face;
You were so adorable and
I couldn't wait to hold you

Thank you for letting me love you the best that I can

A World Without You

I'm certain
the sky wouldn't be blue,
birds wouldn't sing out their melodies,
clouds would gather and be gray
not only in the sky
but in my heart as well;
A world without you
is unimaginable
and god I hope,
unattainable

Golden

I will hold your golden heart with gloves,
for I will not mistreat it;
You are an extraordinary gem,
one that people would fly overseas for,
just to catch a glimpse of it in a crowded room;
People would pay millions just to hear the heartbeat,
Your heart is golden
and your eyes are diamonds
I will always stare in awe

Never forget how incredible you are

My forever is yours

Just know I love you with all my heart

Your Smile

I'm addicted to the way your lips curve at the sides,
lighting a way for your teeth to peer out,
Straight and perfect
as it lights up your eyes;
Your entire face glistens with the happiness
radiating from your heart;
I'm addicted

Thinking Of You

No hour or minute passes
where you're not dancing through my mind,
your toes perfectly pointed,
stance immaculate,
heavenly music softly seeping from the speakers,
You're always there,
front and center,
always on my mind,
always me thinking of you

Different Love

Although we may show our love differently,
I will always try my best
to make you feel loved
and appreciated

Me Time

It's not that I dislike you
or do not love you,
I just need to find my inner peace,
My personal balance once more;
It will keep me aligned with you,
so that I can be the best me
I just need my alone time sometimes
but know
I still love you
I just love me too

Fresh Air

Every day I feel like I have a breath of fresh air;
Because of you
breathing has become a little easier,
my lungs stronger,
breaths softer;
You make me want to wake up every morning
to hear the birds chattering right outside my window;
I feel peace and reassurance;
I feel so damn alive

Come Here

I wish you were in my bed,
with soft breaths,
In and out,
as you dream the sweetest of dreams
while I pull you in close just to feel your warmth;
Thinking I am the luckiest being alive

You're an extraordinary gift;
I cannot fathom how I have you
and you are mine

In all these lifetimes I have known you

Goodnight, My Love

Goodnight my starry-sky eyed girl,
May the warm summer breeze slip through your window
and embrace your body in it's graceful dance,
warming you from head to toe;
Let your eyelids fall heavy
To the wistful movements
and sounds that drift you away to some place magical;
Where you feel love and contentment,
a feeling of which I hope you always feel,
something I will always strive to make for you;
Goodnight my world,
Goodnight my only one,
Goodnight, my love

Afternoon

As the sun hits the porch and reflects off of the stones
I can't help but imagine the way your eyes twinkle
when they look into mine;
I feel the breeze and see the trees sway
I wonder about the way your feet move while you walk
a few steps ahead of me;
I can see a blue sky and puffs of clouds,
I begin to think about how incredible the world is
to be able to be so beautiful,
which always leads me to the baffling thought
of your beauty,
I wonder how something upon this Earth can be even more beautiful and marvelous than the Earth herself

Unfathomable

What it's like to love someone like you,
I cannot explain
for I am speechless in your presence

I will always fight for us,
For our safety
For our love
I will always fight
for you

Never in a million years
would I have imagined coming across someone like you

When I’m with you
I feel connected,
put together,
complete;
When you leave,
my body forgets how to function;
I sit in the silence and think back on the time we shared;
I want you back here in my arms
breathing softly in my ear,
Not hundreds of miles away
just come back to my door
to this moment;
Just come back

You will be enough
when the sun sets and the air goes still,
You will be enough when you're at your worst
when your body aches
and your soul needs rest,
In the moments your hair is up
With makeup smeared along your face from the hard day,
when your voice is shaky
and you want to cry
You will be enough
You are always enough

2:03

Time goes by too fast;
I don't want this to end

As I gaze up at the sky
I become engulfed in its beauty
I think back to you and
how I don't need to see the sky everyday
if those days meant I could look into your eyes
instead

-You Are the Sky

All I can think of tonight,
is you lying next to me

Keep me safe,
from the raging storms within my soul,
to the ones beating upon the horizon;
I feel so safe in your arms,
in your love;
protect me

I pray each night
that I will live to see the day
when your face is smushed into the pillow next to mine
and the sun rising right outside the sheer curtains
of our bedroom window;
I pray to watch you wipe the sleep out of your eyes,
one by one,
I pray my heart will beat on and on
just for me to see you live your life;
Just for me to love each piece of you,
I pray,
I pray,
and I pray for just one more day
by your side

I want to sleep by you,
near you,
next to you;
in your arms

It’s so great to be able to love a person like you

The day you don't have to leave,
will be the day my heart stays full

-It Will Come

Terribly
Terribly
I love you this much
with the force of ten thousand men
The force,
it drives me mad with angst,
It brings me love,
hope,
and trust
The force leads me to you
softly,
calmly,
with swirling winds
and elbow pads
just in case one of us gets scuffed up
only because we love with such a force

My Dear

When you're home and I'm here,
my heart aches with a terrible roaring pain;
for me knowing
I cannot hold you in my arms tonight
makes my body weak
and awakens the waterfalls within;
For I know how lucky I am
but how marked with misery this is;
There is no doubt how great my love for you is
and how strong my heart must be for you to be there
and me to be here
one day,
I will come home to you my dear
one day,
we will come home

You ask me if I think I could wake up to your eyes
every day from here on out
I tell you how unsure I am
about many things
in this complex life
but I think I could use the simplicity of your eyes
each morning to soothe my soul,
I wouldn't want anything else
besides those eyes to start my day

How could I ever live without you

Intertwine with me my love,
for my arms have no home without you

Love,
open up
and let all the sides of you shine,
show me the edges of the divine;
No matter if they are rough and jagged
or smooth like silk;
I will love them with as much as I can give;
These edges are yours,
your edges are mine,
These edges are ours to define

I will love you through everything

Thumb-kiss

Let our fingers glide across the screen,
A hundred miles away;
Let us see the colors
Let us feel the vibrations
Let's feel the closeness of the distance;
Through our screens
Seeping red into our hearts;
The reminder of the start,
Straight from our hearts

No matter how hard this gets
No matter how sad I am
because I can't hold you at night;
I promise it won't stop me
from swimming oceans
and climbing hills to love you
I promise I won't let the battle tear me apart
from the inside out;
There's no way I will ever stop reaching for you
at the tops of the mountains,
I won't let the distance divide us,
I promise I won't and
I never will

-I'll Be Here

I've never felt so sensitive towards someone before;
I mean this as,
everything you do makes me feel;
I feel the heaviness on your shoulders;
I can touch the waves in your eyes
Almost like our feelings are connected
Tied together,
every move you make,
I mimic,
An emotional connection
I've never felt;
You make me care

Within you,
I have found my eternity.

ABOUT THE AUTHOR

SMR is a passionate person with hopes that people can feel seen within their work. She resides alongside her puppy, Margot, and is always creating.

www.ingramcontent.com/pod-product-compliance
Lightning Source LLC
LaVergne TN
LVHW091305150826
845673LV00006B/1538

9798847587426